W9-BUK-537

Dear Fred

By Susanna Rodell   *Illustrated by* Kim Gamble

TICKNOR & FIELDS BOOKS FOR YOUNG READERS
New York 1995

First American edition 1995 published by
Ticknor & Fields
Books for Young Readers
A Houghton Mifflin company, 215 Park Avenue South,
New York, New York 10003

Text copyright © 1994 by Susanna Rodell
Illustrations copyright © 1994 by Kim Gamble

First published in Australia by Penguin Books Australia Ltd

All rights reserved. For information about permission to reproduce
selections from this book, write to Permissions, Houghton Mifflin Company,
215 Park Avenue South, New York, New York 10003.

Manufactured in Australia
Book design by Cathy van Ee
The text of this book is set in 22pt. Bembo
The illustrations are watercolor on Arches paper, reproduced in full color

10 9 8 7 6 5 4 3 2 1

Library of Congress Cataloging-in-Publication Data

Rodell, Susanna
Dear Fred / by Susanna Rodell;
illustrated by Kim Gamble.
p.   cm.
Summary: A young girl writes a letter to her half brother back in
Australia telling him how much she misses him.
ISBN 0-395-71544-X
[1. Brothers and sisters-Fiction. 2. Divorce-Fiction.
3. Letters-Fiction.] I. Gamble, Kim, ill. II. Title.
PZ7.R61De 1995
[E]-dc20 94-19926 CIP AC

To Besha, Fred, Grace and Ruby — S.R.

To Greer — K.G.

Dear Fred,
I am still missing you.

When we went away, I didn't know it would
be this long. Mom says it's been almost a year.
It feels funny that you're not here. Mom says
you're still my brother and you will always be
my brother, even though you're far away.

She says she misses you, too. She says that's the kind of thing that happens in complicated families like ours.

I like my school here in America. I have two
new friends, Jessica and Jacob. They come to
my house to play.

I remember, back home in Australia, when it was our turn to have you at our house, we used to play every day after school. I never thought of you as my half brother, even though you had a different dad. The weeks you stayed with him, I always missed you. Nobody else had time to play with me.

I liked it when we played knights and
dragons. You always let me be the queen

and you would be my knight. I got to order
you around and you called me "Your Majesty."

My favorite was when we made mud
banquets on your stove in the backyard.
You were such a good cook. We made big
stews and you let me stir them. We put in
ashes from the barbecue and grass and berries.

We made beautiful cakes and decorated
them with fuchsia flowers and pretty leaves.
We made mud tea and everybody would
come out and pretend to eat.

We don't have a backyard here.

Sometimes you got angry at me.

I was little then, and you said everyone
thought I was the cute one and you
were just a kid. You got in trouble if
I cried. You said it wasn't fair.

Well, now Ruby's the cute one and
everybody's always going all googly-woogly
over her, and I'm just a kid.

She's just learned how to walk.
I've known how to walk for ages.

Sometimes Ruby eats my crayons.

Once I saved her life in the bathtub.
She fell over and her face was in the
water and I pulled her up.

Mom says I'm a good sister, but it's hard
being the only big kid in the house.

I wish you were here to help.

Mom says you'll come over at Christmastime.
I can't wait. We could go skating and build
a snowman.

Ruby's okay, really.
I think you'd like her. She's very soft.

I'm bigger now. When you're
here, I promise I won't cry.

If you get in trouble, I'll get in
trouble, too. It'll be fair.

Mom wrote this down for me.
I told her what to say.

I love you, Freddy,
and I hope you remember me.

Love, Grace . . .

NOV 25 1995

SHELTER ROCK PUBLIC LIBRARY

3 1324 00299 3522

E R
R

Rodell, Susanna.

Dear Fred.